BETTER LOOKING

CATHERINE VALLEROY

DEDICATION

I dedicate this book to all who have been traumatized and are seeking a spiritual path in order to find their authentic selves.

TABLE OF CONTENTS

ACKNOWLEDGMENTS

I would like to acknowledge Brandon Vick for shooting another amazing cover that captures my authenticity as a woman in my fifties.

I would also like to thank Sam Mulcahey and Wendy Lista for their help with proofreading.

INTRODUCTION

Better Looking is the second book of three I have written as I continue to seek out authenticity in my life. My first book, *Better Look*, chronicled the start of my journey inward by sharing my struggles and successes in my marriage, motherhood, and a corporate career. *Better Looking*, picks up as my marriage was ending, I was profoundly struggling with mental illness, was no longer able to work, and started to acknowledge having been through a lot of trauma in my life.

Better Looking takes the reader through more milestones of even deeper introspections. Not only does it suggest that I am getting to know myself even better, but that I am coming to accept myself more wholistically. The growth I have experienced in this time of my life has brought me closer to my truest emotional, spiritual, and physical self. Within this time frame, I began developing a growing comfort with myself. I can honestly say I found myself as beautiful, if not more so, shooting the cover for the second book. In that sense I saw myself as *better-looking*.

In *Better Looking*, the first poems are very intentionally placed. They give a chronology marking my struggles to: own my beauty as I age, accept the ending of my marriage, work through sexual abuse, and come to love myself and others again. The placement of the rest of the poems is fairly random, but not without themes. A big theme for me was to describe my spiritual path. A lot of my poems have to do with the breath and how many times I equate that with my understanding of a power greater than myself. Whether it be the breath, nature, or relationships, all of these things are remarkably linked to forming a God of my understanding. A lesser theme that runs throughout the book is to voice how COVID affected me. I also engage in some introspection about Black Lives Matter as well as the political climate of the United States. This is because a lot of this book was written in the early 2020's.

Much to my delight, I also explored writing haiku and senryu in *Better Looking*. Both types of poems have three lines with 5-7-5 syllables. Haiku tends to be about nature and serious subject matter. It can be described as contemplative. Senryu is more humorous and satirical, poking fun at the absurdities of human behavior. And finally, there

is a journal, my signature feature of the books in this series. Hopefully, this will entice you, the reader, to record your own journey to finding your truest self.

The first two books pay special attention to how I look at myself and life, following me on my journey inward. Many of the poems written in *Better Looking* come from my practice of stream of consciousness after meditating. I have run a sangha for 11 years, where we center ourselves through prayer and meditation and then journal about what has bubbled up to the surface. More often than not, I write a poem. In my first two books I am looking for and at myself to glean my unique place in this world. The final book, *Seeing*, is about no longer looking for myself, but coming to a place of truly seeing who I am, the final step toward authenticity. It is the process of coming to truly know who you are. *Seeing*, will be coming out sometime in December of 2025.

Welcome to *Better Looking* and enjoy your seeking!

BODY IMAGE

I entertain loathing—
Within every window and mirror
I reflect.
Am I distorted?
Am I dishonest?
Why do I look with disdain at myself?
What if I were to forego this shaming?
What if I became willing to look beyond my external self?
Wouldn't I then find the inner beauty
Of my own love?

Beauty is full.
It is of itself,
And everything is of it.
It shines.
It cleanses.
It illuminates.
It is within
And out.
It is under
And around.
It is words
And rays
And flowers.
It is laughter,
And tears,
And moons.
It rises as something sets.
It is everywhere
And everything is of it.
So, I beg of you
To see it,
Look at it,
Be it.
For it is the truth.

THE SEPARATION

I understand that our love is complicated.
We are damaged souls.
We have limitations.
Most couples do.
I know in our hearts we do not see the other as unworthy of
love.
Although it sometimes seems that way.
We both get scared
Especially on days born out of
Complications, unpredictability, confusion, dis-ease.
And we fiercely clash-
Fighting for love and reassurance.
"But who has the time?"
But to save us, shouldn't we take all the time in the world?
Yet you run out the door overwhelmed by one more thing,
I slam the door doubting your capacity to commit the way I
do.
It seems that our past and self-serving expectations
Are always one step ahead of us.
We both turn to other things to help us feel vital.
Me to: God, friends, groups, strangers, therapists-
I share my accusations and observations with them.
I crave what feels like serenity in their support.
Yet true serenity comes to me in those rare moments of
solitude and introspection
When I forget myself and forgive us both.
You seek authoritative, father figures, projects, and jobs
In an effort to regain order in your life.
You think these things are straight forward and run by the
rules of logic.
You bob and weave beyond the expectations of the situation,
In return for tangibles:
Compensation, sound advice,
Education, authorization,
Promotions, a refurbished object,

But still seem deeply unsatisfied.
We both have souls:
They afford us the opportunity to give each other material
and spiritual gifts,
Neither type is wrong or mutually exclusive.
For you put a roof over our heads,
And I made our house a home.
But two souls are never one.
In love they can travel, but frequently they journey alone.
And if we are self-centered in fear and isolation,
We will be impeded from going on.
That is when we have little or nothing to gain with each
other.
Yet no one can make their soul perfect.
All we can do is to keep progressing
Toward creating more peace and clarity within ourselves
And try to share it.
You and I have shared these connections of peace and clarity.
There have been perfect moments
When you have recognized me as Mother Earth-
Carrying and holding life.
I have experienced you as Father Earth-
Strong and protective.
And when we truly come together these things unite.
But, for now, we must work apart
And then together,
To accept and move beyond the pain, mistrust, poor choices
and the unmet expectations
Of our distant and current past.
Can we accept that we will need to be taught new skills and
utilize new tools
Without which we will inevitably go backwards?
Will we then move forward, or stay hopelessly stuck?
Will we finally let our souls unfold,
Sharing the rest of our lifetime celebrating their beauty and
splendor?
Or will we not?

THE STUFF OF MY LOVE'S PAST

In a closet
In 2 drawers
On a nightstand
Is what was left of me.
I come to collect myself.
I come to collect those final bits.
I have done this before.
And now I put them in a box again,
My car again.
But this time I will leave the keys
And walk away.

ERASING

You can't erase me.
You can take down my pictures.
You can throw away the gifts I gave you.
You can repress your memories of me.
But, you can't erase me.
Yet I can lose myself.
I can let the past endlessly torment me.
I can constantly wonder about what could have been.
I can choose not to forgive.
I can blame myself.
So, you see only I can erase me.
Yet, now in my deepest sadness,
I am stronger still without you,
I will come full circle despite the loss,
And I will not be erased.

SLEEP

I fear sleep,
Not because it is like death,
But because you will arouse me
And then steal my innocence.
You are gone,
But to me you are still as a thief.
For as I start to drift off to sleep,
Even now,
There is a painful apprehension
That you will come.
And just as my moment of peace should be descending
You will thrust it away,
And try to awaken in me a woman
When I am only a child.

    l. Coping
Wishing a child's simple dream
To be in the clouds
For freedom is there—
Then reality…
The mind comes back.
The respite short
then over.
Oh, but I will dream of clouds again
That sacred place of survival.

    II. Thriving
To go beyond clouds
To be grounded at last.
With thoughts of the moment
Not of the past.
Remembering without
Having to stare.
Accepting that life
Is not always fair.
The truth is bitter
Of that I concur.
Yet working through it
Is best I assure.
Reflecting on actions
Did more than survive.
Now I resurrect
And come willingly
To thrive.

NO NEED FOR JUDGEMENT DAY

What is the importance of all the good or bad things we have
done
or have been done to us in our lifetime's?
And do we wonder this,
hoping we attained and bared enough to go to heaven?
Perhaps we will come to know someday,
When we grab the knob of our last door,
Turning it quickly to see which absolute is on the other side:
Pure light
Or pure darkness.
Yet what if there is neither:
Pure light,
Nor pure emptiness,
But all the love and fulfillment that alluded us in life?
What if, throughout our lives,
We remembered the many Gifts and Lessons that were
bestowed upon us?
And what if we had grown to be a better person because of
them?
What if we did more than ask for forgiveness—
But profoundly changed our characters and repented?
Would there then be the need for Judgment Day?

I am trying to recollect
The pieces of myself,
To reassemble
the essence of
my hope,
my reason,
my heart,
my soul.
So, I pray for
Insight,
Foresight,
Freedom from this hardship.
Yet, I now wonder if
I am too proud
To receive grace.
And then the Universe opens
To reassemble
And direct me again.
But rebirth is
A hard blessing,
For life is profound suffering.
Yet one can turn,
With exquisite acceptance,
This suffering into peace.
For I have now come to see
How hardships
Are the pathway
To peace.

AFFAIR OF THE HEART

In the absence of love
The heart reluctantly beats
Longing and regrets
And hope.
It pumps
With resolve
To stay the course
Pulsing life
And depletion
And life again.
With the mind
Love is but a concept.
With the heart
Love rises and falls as a feeling.
Between these two
Is consent.
Take love for what it is worth then:
A small ransom,
A hefty fine,
The lottery.

DREAM CATCHER

Would it be
That you will let me catch your dreams.
For if you do,
I promise I will come to know them
Dearly in my heart.
I would let them shine,
Their tails streaming brightly,
Their dust falling upon you.
Let me be as your North Star
Giving back to you authenticity from your longings.
Let me come to know you well enough to be your muse.
Trust me,
For that if you do,
I will appreciate that such an act
Is braver than love.

NEW LOVERS

Our friction combusts
The freedom of new lovers
Becomes fire.

DISTANCE

There is a distance,
A distinct chink in our amore.
We have held each other with words and thoughts.
We have held each other in dreams,
But never have we held each other.

Hold your breath
And submerge.
For the path is deep and blue and full.
It surrounds you
As God does.
Love is divine.
Love is beyond knowing.
Love is beyond the mere mind's reach.
It is depth, and breadth, and width.
It fills and turns the earth.
Infinity is not beyond its reach.
And so, I dreamed this dream for us.
I dreamed this dream for you.
Then awoke to find
I must first know these things
Within myself.

RELATIONSHIP

That distance between
Our heaven and earth—
Is it profound?
Is it measurable?
Are steps the path
That will lead us to each other,
So that we may walk hand in hand
Not feet apart,
Miles apart,
Lifetimes apart,
Salvations apart.
From a distance I can only
Think of how I will know you,
My best guess all I have for now…
To close my eyes and suppose.
But someday is not always enough.
Yet perhaps our words and thoughts will gather us up.
So until then, in patient times,
Let us kindly, observantly
Ponder each other.

In the depths of a union,
We can come together,
Each deeply abiding the other,
Our truest souls
Expanding toward heaven.
And then a contemplative love
Will be our gift.

DELICIOUS

When something is delicious
It is lush and fragrant
To the taste.
It is after all an explosion
Of thoughts
And buds
And honest assessments.
It is hilarious
And serious,
Popping bubbles
Squirting them
Into another's dream.
Imagine
A taste
Imagine
A texture
Imagine
A porcelain plate
And cut into
The sensual delight
Of this meal
We call
LIFE!

CINDERELLA

The mundane seems bleak.
You cook, you clean, and yet you
Are Cinderella!

DESPAIR

Cold, dull hopelessness
Comes to my deep flesh and dreams
Longingly, I hope.

PROOF OF LIFE

A symphony of proof—
Life sighs unfolding
Crescendo, decrescendo,
Staccato, legato.
Its truth exists in its opposites.
Sometimes life plays dissonantly,
Sometimes sweetly—
Its movements directed by notes,
The outcome music,
A proof of life.

MANIA

I love the kinetics of it,
The careless projection
Into dreams
I would otherwise
Never have had.
The energy
That revs
My engine
To explode fuel
Into speed.
And "Ah!"
It's all about speed.
Faster, faster!
Adrenaline and excitement
Beyond ecstasy.
But even a racehorse
Cannot keep accelerating.
It can however,
maintain its fastest pace.
Yet my pace is
Too fast to maintain.
Therefore, I fall down before the finish-line
That was fancied in an elaboration
Of my dis—ease.

PATIENT FORGIVENESS

Patient forgiveness is what we truly need.
Yet we sit with anxious moments so often
That we cannot remember peace.
We carry despair.
We drink the poison of lies.
We think there is only optionless suffering.
But then the light of the spirit is bestowed upon our
darkness,
And sin, sadness, and remorse fade away.
At last forgiveness transcends the boundaries of life's cold
instances.
Remember that God is pure love,
Pure forgiveness
And that we were created in that image.

GIDEON

Why carry only
Half the message when God
Is both Old and New?

DISASSOCIATION

If you only knew how dimensionless the landscape is to me,
The landscape of your face and lit buildings at night.
How I long to see the world as you do,
In all its circumstances:
Dynamic, full, and bright.
Once I stepped into a dangerous world
With no place to hide, but in the recesses of my mind.
And how deeply I drilled into them,
Only to find myself vulnerable.
Oh, and my tensely dysmorphic body….
"Close your eyes little girl and what do you see?"
"Not even an outline of me…."
But him—
Abandonment,
Abuse,
Hell on earth.
"And now why do you carry a basket of posies?"
'I am seeking to give them away,
An offering
To the shadows,
So that I might truly see my world and me again!'

DEAR BREATH

Come to me Dear Breath
For you are as God.
Filled with you
I rise and fall with no end to beginnings.
You give me hope Dear Breath
As you are the source that sustains me.
My constant companion,
Loyal and abundant,
Never do I call upon you
For you were there first,
And will be there last.
Amen

EMPTINESS

When I silence my mind there is infinity.
Broad expanses of nothing
Yet there in is everything:
Light yet no light,
The presence of self,
The absence of self.
Fly little bird to no destination.
Fly just to fly.

MOVING ON

Trapped with thoughts of you
Couldn't get out of my head
Till another came.

OFFERINGS

These simple things
I give to thee offerings:
My heart beating,
My eyes blinking,
The air as it passes into me.
When I am mindful
These simple things
Are my soul's connection
To You

THE ELEVATOR AT ONE ELEVEN

We ride together
Me and my thoughts
Mostly with young men
Asian musicians
Black women in their wigs and weaves….
Diverse diversions
From my heavy bags of groceries
Going up,
My overflowing laundry
Going down.
"Hello" I say,
"How are you today?"
"Go to Eastman?"
"You look lovely."
Each word
Each question
Each statement
Trying to make a connection
And is always met with shy eye contact, or
surprise.
Either way we are all equally guilty
Of pushing buttons
As this ship rises and falls
On the waves of uneven weights and pullies.
Then in seconds,
"This is me"
(third floor).
"Have a good day."
"A blessed day."
Said only to the black women,
'Know this white girl means no colloquial disrespect,'
I am only trying to connect.
The door opens
Leaving behind
Shy eye contact and surprise.

Either way
The passage was safe
A connection made
On this
One of the many, short journeys
In a life's moment.
I get off,
The door closes,
And I make my way back to my apartment.

OF THE BREATH

Thoughts come,
My feelings revelated.
I come to see the truth of
The moment
By transcending myself,
By fixing my life to the breath.
I am of the breath
I am a breath in god's universe.
From the air I breathe
With my limitations and
Greatest feats.
I feast on the air,
Abundance abounds.
And I am never left alone,
For the breath is always with me,
And the breath is God.

AUTUMN APPROACHES

The cusp of summer
Is drawing upon autumn.
As one retracts,
The other expands.
The air to my left is heated
To my right holds a faint chill.
There is a yellow jacket by my feet.
He knows his days of pollen
Are numbered.
And I am pensive that
He might sting me.
I am aware of these subtle changes,
As autumn approaches.

CODEPENDENCY

I cannot help but be a barometer.
I rise and fall
With every supposition of you.
If you look at me sideways
My heart sinks.
If you are angry
I assume it is my fault.
If you have needs
I seek to fulfill
Them all.
I stretch myself thin,
By choice,
Thinking I should pay the price
For our relationship.

FALLING IN LOVE

Hold your breath
And submerge.
The path is deep, and blue, and full.
It surrounds you, as God does.
Love is divine.
Love is beyond knowing.
Love is beyond the mere mind's reach.
It is depth
And breadth
And width.
It fills and turns the earth.
Infinity is not beyond its bounds.
And so, I dreamed this dream with you.
I dreamed this dream for us.
And I awoke to find first
Love for myself.

NIGHTTIME'S DREAM

Hope for the moon to spill over you.
Its milky pearls upon your skin
Divulging beyond the shadows
Truths once hidden
As you succumb to dreaming.
Come to be lit with the night's spectrum of
Black and grey and white.
The scene is:
Cool and solemn,
Sweet and haunting—
Sleepy.

PRINCIPLES

We put the story
Out of sight,
Black Live's Matter
Worth no fight?
Unhappy Republic
Struggles to survive.
From liberty and justice
We do not derive.
Indivisible Union
Will soon be left.
Principles of equality
Completely bereft.
This nation will be lost
Without a soul,
Unless those at the helm
Surrender control.

MINDFUL

My body comes
To the breath
As a foreigner.
Mindful thoughts
Take me to a place
Of reckoning.
How heavy
I was
When I first
Came to stop:
How torn,
And regretful,
And hollow.
Now I am grateful
For simplicity.
Now I breathe
To become freedom.

The essence of time is subtle.
It meanders as a river.
Thoughtfully it carves gentle curves.
Tumultuously it rushes unimpeded.
I stand on its banks.
I stand in currents rough and sedate.
I hear the echoes of its different travels.
The river
Follows the obstacles of rocks,
Rubbing their surfaces smooth.
Perhaps then the river's run will flow further
Perhaps then it will gather to be still.

GRACE

I draw from flowers
Sweet nectar to make honey.
God's grace is golden!

PERFUME

A lovely fragrance
Holds the dewy remembrance
Of another day

MOMENTS

The best moments pause
To find themselves.
They patiently attend
To the life around them.
We are moments in God's Universe.
We are a piece of its vast holiness.
Whether you conceive of a moment
As great or small,
Powerful or meek,
Painful or joyous,
A moment is just that,
A moment.

HIGH SUMMER

The sun melts
The day
Leaving
Nowhere to hide.
Even under a tree,
The air hangs heavily
Without the luxury
Of a breeze.
To all this
The body responds,
Weeping tears
Of sweat.
All stays in
Humid suspension
Even after
The rain.
Just another
High summer day
In Memphis.

Give focus to the sublime
And wonder if we will dance later.
Illuminate your understanding
And bare the truth.
For all this may come to be only our imagination
Or perhaps the future of our mind's eye.

How many dark days
Before the rising of hope?
With unity—few…

COFFEE

Its granules bathe
In the hiss and gurgle of water,
Run over
Again and again
With the proposition to take
Both into a union—
A smooth
Strong
Brown elixir.
How do I relay its perfume?
From the oils of the bean's fruit
That make this drink essential.
Finally, the swish of steaming fluid
That whirls its circumference
Around the cup,
Settling into a glorious bath for
My patient taste buds,
Sleepy brain,
Glasses to fog.
I take mine pure
No milk or sugar to embezzle the experience.
Ah, and now I draw upon this delight
That makes my lips plump and supple,
That draws the temperature of my mouth to rise,
That warms my throat and chest as a blanket would,
And I become a pilgrim of sips.

KNOWLEDGE

Pain is a part of
The fruit that Eve gave Adam.
Knowledge must be pain.

DO BLACK LIVES MATTER?

Poignant Black voices
Have come to a fever pitch.
Yet they're still shackled.

LADY IN WAITING

I do not
Long for you.
For when you leave,
You gently place me
In waiting.
My heart full,
I patiently stand,
To mark your return.

THE NOTIFIER

Heavy are the words
That this soldier must speak
Announcing to another
The beginning of their sorrow.
How the soldier must stand in waiting
From the knock on the door,
To its opening.
To watch eyes well
With the anticipated expectation of this moment.
The guttural scream
Exposes this now endless abyss.
The notifier turns to walk away,
Knowing that the recipient will never reach the ground again,
Whilst they will never stop hearing the sounds of war.

Time is fluid
And crisp.
Time is a reflection,
A percussion,
A release.
Time is forever,
Never to an end.
Time is young and ancient in
The same breath,
The same water,
The same air,
The same fire.
Time is of the earth
Of the universe
Of the most divine.
It is received.
It is given.
Therefore are we
Not time?

TAMBERLAIN FARM

The farm stretches deeply
Into the woods
Across the fields.
It is abundant.
Its fertility comes
To many animals
Plentiful crops.
There is devotion there.
A mother suckles her kittens,
A cow chews its cud.
The corn stalks bend to the wind.
A family sits to grace and dinner.
Their memories collect,
Grandparents, parents, children, their children's children,
Bless this place.
On it goes through generations,
A legacy of the heart,
Tamberlain.

LOVE MAKING

You fill my lips with blood,
plumping them for our feast.
Flesh to flesh,
The dewy extremities of
Lust and love entwine.
The thrust of embraces
That part and rejoin,
And oh how ecstasy comes
To play its lovely music upon us.
Enjoy this sweet escape from life's drudgery.
Enjoy the holy Palmer's Kiss.
Enjoy this Denouement of pleasure's falling.

Long before this, my home held me like a prisoner
Forcing this caged animal to commit mental illness.
Yet time has passed
And I fall into the bosom of guidance,
The requiem to self-forgiveness,
Self-love,
Freedom.
But now the world has stopped,
Its feverish pace on all plains halted,
And I realize I still have cause to delve deeper.
Hadn't I been awaiting all along for this kind of permission,
To go beyond self
To commune with a holy pause.
For therein lies my soul's work.
Therein is my cause.
Therein is the path to my continuing salvation.

MAGRITTE'S CHAPS

Bowlers and apples
Making green and obscure chaps
In his floating world.

A country lined with bread and circuses
Seduces the parade,
Its crowd.
A battle really
A battle for principals
And spirit
And lives.
We are polar in our assumptions.
We are lost at each other's expense.
We are parting with so much
As we gain
Nothing.
Mourn America
For instead of unity
We have trenches.

CIRCUMSTANCES

All circumstances
That are beyond our control
Are held in God's grace.

LOVE'S FANTASY

My thoughts beg I go further ahead
To an imagined future
Before what the truth of us can be.
I am driven to choreograph
Our love making
A walk in the park
Conversations.
In my reality's dream
I make bets against the odds of a daisy,
Plucking petals to the end of,
"He loves me!"
Yet isn't this only the outcome of an imagined flower?
Not the strength and breath of days,
Or time.
And isn't TIME:
This I Must Earn!

RESPITE

Seek respite
Dear traveler
And forge your destiny along the road
another time.
Stop dear traveler
Enjoy the nature that you have put aside.
Take heart dear traveler
Life is a journey
Of many destinations.
Stop dear traveler.
Lay your head upon my bosom
And enjoy the peace of rest
For tomorrow the road will still be there.

DISTANCE

There as a distance
A distinct chink in our amore.
We held each other with words and thoughts.
We held each other in dreams,
But never held each other.

IN THE BREATH

In the breath
There is a releasing.
My body unfolds
Its tense possessions
Fear, projection, what if…..
In the breath
There is a cleansing
Like waves of summer breezes
That wash over my body.
Breathe
Unfold
Release
Peace.

SWEET NOTHINGS

In the silence
There were sweet nothings.
Our heat vibrated as we drew closer.
What would it mean to embrace now?
What would a kiss mean?
Perhaps the sweetness of nothing—
Perhaps once inaudible hearts
Beating together
As one.

MANIC

An impulse lit off
Fireworks in my blank brain
And they exploded

ESCAPING THE TRAP

The framework of a trap
Is the mind going without check,
Wandering the landscape
Without purposeful direction.
With some hope,
With some determination
Wanderings turn to journeys
And the soul is called upon by life
To move toward ends
That do justify their means,
Disposing mere faith
For true Divinity.

The truest love is
Beyond words,
For it is DIVINE.
When we love
We are without darkness,
And all at once enlightened.
And our minds and bodies
Navigate
The complex
Simplicity
Of the state
Of love
We are in.

THE SLAP

The first slap pink,
Kinder than the black and blue ones.
Either way you cry.

THE PROFOUND

It is not always complicated truths,
But simple beauty that enlightens us.
It expands our insight,
Our glory,
Our dreams.
When one seeks
To stop
To look
To listen for it—
The difficult meaning of life,
All at once
Becomes kind.

THE SUBTLETIES OF SNOWFLAKES

Speak only of white
As they gesture the wind's song.
What dream is this
that leaves diamonds behind.
Sweeping clean the landscape
Floating before rest
One upon another
Conforming.

UNDERPINNINGS

Unhook the girdle,
Trying to fit into Spanks…
Where do we go next?

MY BREATH MANIFESTS

Real time
Real moments.
With each breath
There is a rising
Then falling
And between these two
Are instances of when I truly am.
I sit within beginnings
And endings
And seem to notice
Life is between them.
Between them is common ground
For me to lay upon.
And what comes is the peace of taking on life
And then letting go of it.

THE SUMMER SKY

Gazing at the sky
I interpret floating things,
The sun and morphed clouds,
A rainbow.
Dreamed as if a dream;
Hold it dearly,
Let it pass—
Recall it later.
Think of this as heaven;
How it brings you through the darkness
Its sight is a promise
To recollect on grey days.

THE WOODS

The woods are my cathedral.
A sacred calm is there.
In them I pay homage to the God within me,
For the character of the woods calls it out.
With the kiss of its wind—
A summer's brush,
A winter's bite,
One finds solace.
I go deep into the woods
But before it closes over me
I gaze upon the clouds or stars
Letting the rays of the day
Or moonlight
Wash over me.
Then there is the fragrance of sap,
The freshness of greenery
The decay of leaves.
I walk further in silence to hear its sounds.
Always I walk fervently
To lose myself
In its Holy Infinity.

WAITING

I wait in silence
Patiently for the phone to ring
Your voice brings music.

SLEEP

The cat lays sprawling
I am wrapped tightly fetal
Night surrounds our dreams…

DREAMS

Imagine life
As a billowing dream,
Its tendrils fluttering
In an elegant wind,
Its sounds
Opaque and crystal.
Oh, that I should live my dreams—
That I should have them
In my heart
And move them
Into actions
That would thicken the agar
To grow still more dreams
Of love and charity and hope,
Dreams lead by the compass and sexton and North Star,
Dreams that begin and pause and end
To dream.

THE SURFACE

The surface is above it all
The top of the water
The top of the earth
All at once
It can be flat or rocky,
Calm or agitated,
Pleasant or unfriendly.
It is the state of things here and coming,
Things building and in ruins,
Things that grow and die…
The surface is where life bursts through
To pass time and return
To the apparent end of days
That harken life to reach for the surface again
From its dark rebirth beneath.

Our friction combusts
The freedom of ripe lovers
Becomes a fire.

FUNDAMENTAL BREATH

My breath is fundamental.
It is the essence of my being.
With it I expand the universe.
Yet when I am caught in life's drudgery,
By my fears and impatience,
It seems as though I am breathless.
Yet there is great hope
when I take on life's circumstances
One breath at a time.
Rejuvenated with the next inhale and exhale,
Each breath becomes a rebirth,
A resurrection.

THE COMING

I will know you
By your actions,
Your words,
The sentiment of your gestures.
You won't posture against
The deeply held principles
In your heart.
You will walk the straight line
Of truth and hope,
Willing to risk all,
As few do.
All resonate with me,
You are in my mind's eye…
When will you come?

OUR LOVE

Despite the distance between us
Our love is already deep.
It longs
Then tempers that longing
With great hope.
Our love is kind.
It does not seem to struggle
with cruelty and defensiveness.
Already it provides
understanding and tenderness.
But there too
Is reticence
Along with the savoring
Of each day.
Someday,
You will come to me
Openly,
With resolve.
And I will accept you,
With all my heart,
With all my soul.
Then our longings
And misgivings
Will cease.
And we will truly unite.
And our truth
Will be our love.

When I transcend all feelings
A comfortable numbness will overcome me
And I will disappear into nothing.
In nothing there will be everything.
An abundance of frivolous dancing
To less than music
More than sound.
The juice of dawn's
Bulbous horizon
Will bleed pink and yellow and orange
Into clouds of blue and white.
I will see across my life
To the truth of days
Where angels had shed
God's tears for me
And caught them as rainbow covenants
For my salvation.
I will awaken from this dream of life
And know that I have lived.

MY PEACEFUL BREATH

I am nourished by the peace of my breath.
For with each one comes a freedom
from time passing to quickly
and too slowly.
When I engage in the counting of each breath,
When I trust that that is enough,
There is a gift of a clear mind,
A free mind,
And so an infinite landscape of nothing is everything,
This respite from the clutter of thoughts.

MEDITATION

When I silence my mind,
There is infinity.
Broad expanses of nothing
Yet there in is everything:
Light
Yet no light,
The presence of self,
The absence of self,
Awareness
And blindness,
Agility
And frailty.
So, fly little bird to no destination.
Fly to fly. . .

ST. FRANCIS

Emptiness fulfills
"How could that be?", he once said.
"You are not alone!"

BREATHING

My stillness is resilient.
It seeks strength
In every up and down
In and out of my breathing.
I came to sit with discomfort
I came to sit with dis-ease,
And each breath beckoned me to peace.
The shift came
When I engaged with the breath and lived it.
Then I left behind
The damage of unrequited hope
And returned to my truest self.

OUR RELATIONSHIP

At the beginning of our relationship
There was a distance between
Our heaven and earth—
Had it been profound?
Was it measurable?
Were steps the path
That led us to each other,
So that we could walk hand in hand
Not feet apart,
Miles apart,
Lifetimes apart,
Salvations apart.
From a distance I can only
Think of how I would know you,
My best guess all I had…
To close my eyes and suppose
Somedays was not always enough.
For it was the words and thoughts that gathered us up
Toward our possible domain.
Until then, with patience,
We kindly, observantly
Pondered each other.

GRACE

There is in grace
Great comfort.
For it floats
Off tongues
And fingers.
It moves effortlessly
Across the Universe.
It is the comet's tail,
The ballerina on point,
Rings that embrace the water's surface.

That word really spins
A gyroscope can't do it
Better than a child.

Catherine's Poetic Life

In the breath
There is a releasing.
My body unfolds
Its tense possessions
Fear, projection, what if…..
In the breath
There is a cleansing
Like waves of summer breezes
That wash over my body.
Breathe
Unfold
Release
Peace.

WILLINGNESS

I delight in the willingness of my open heart.
For through it, I have come to know the God within.
To be willing
Is to be honest.
To try,
Is to work.
To have an open heart
Is to let the dawn's light fill you,
So that you are warm with others and yourself.
Delight in going beyond existence
To the richness of all that you are,
And as you continue,
All that you will be.

PARTING THOUGHTS

I think, dress, decorate, cook, create, and meditate poetically. Living poetically means that I am constantly expressing my imagination by bringing it to fruition through my actions. In doing so, I believe I live mindfully. In doing so, I believe I am manifesting my truest form and life.

I started writing poetry when I was 8 years old. Even back then, I found doing so was a delightful release and an important form of self-expression. Writing of all kinds is still very important to me.

Over the past 20 years, I have worked on three books of poetry: *Better Look, Better Looking,* and *Seeing.*

I have also begun two books of Prose: *Humble Food* and *Meditations from the Stone Soup Sangha* and a children's book, *Need Love.*

What follows is your opportunity to express yourself and start recording your journey inward. I have included a journal for you to *better look* at who you are. You don't have to be a poet per se; just be honest. Use your words, for they are magical, transformative, and empowering. They are one of the most important vehicles you have in this life that will release you to be yourself. The angel now serves you. For this is your poetic life.

JOURNAL

Live Your Life Poetically

Catherine Valleroy is a poet who has been writing verse since the tender age of eight. Her work, which is deeply personal and introspective, reflects her path toward self-awareness and authenticity. Because she is moved by all things natural and spiritual, she considers herself a spiritual poet.

Her first book, *Better Look*, tells the reader about her twenty-year journey of self-disclosure and spiritual growth. The premise of her second book, *Better Looking*, is that her journey of self-disclosure has now taken an even deeper dive into self-awareness. In her final book, *Seeing*, the reader comes to understand that the author's journey is no longer about looking at herself but about coming to see who she truly is.

In addition, Catherine is working on two books of Prose: *Humble Food* and *Meditations from the Stone Soup Sangha* and a children's book, *Need Love*.

In conjunction with writing, Catherine runs a sangha, referred to as her **Stone Soup Sangha**. Eleven years ago, she began this sangha by drawing from three things: The Serenity Prayer, Zazen, and stream of consciousness journaling. As more people joined other meditative practices were incorporated: ringing of the heart chakra bell, drawing tarot cards, a spiritual reading and discussion, and setting intentions before closing. Catherine does this work with recovery groups including a halfway house for ex-offenders, supportive living programs, and gap year students. She also runs private groups out of her home.

Catherine lives in Upstate New York and attended Hiram College for a year before transferring to SUNY Geneseo, where she graduated in 1987 with a BA in Political Science and a minor in Communications. She credits both schools with nurturing her poetic prowess.

www.ingramcontent.com/pod-product-compliance
Lightning Source LLC
Chambersburg PA
CBHW040834010826
48978CB00012BB/755